MY GRANDMA LIVES AT THE AIRPORT

Published by Red Hill Press
PO Box 2053
Carbondale, CO 81623

Publisher's Cataloging-in-Publication Data
Rudner, Rebecca.
My grandma lives at the airport / Rebecca Rudner.–Carbondale, CO: Red Hill Press, 2002.

    p.   ;   cm.
    SUMMARY: a look at keeping families together and connected when they live
     far apart.
    ISBN 0-9708217-0-0
    1. Family-Juvenile fiction. 2. Grandparents-Juvenile fiction. 3.
Grandparent and child-Juvenile fiction. 4. Family-Fiction. I. Title.

| PS3618.U364 M94 | 2002 | 2001086749 |
| 813.6 [E] | –dc21 | CIP |

06 05 04 03 02 • 5 4 3 2 1

Project coordination by Jenkins Group, Inc. • www.bookpublishing.com
Photo Credit Cy Jones Badger Photography
Illustrations by Leroy Morvant
Book design by Kelli Leader

Printed in Singapore

In memory of
Lillian Barash Rudner & Elvira Fratesi Failla

Shelby flew out of bed. "Mommy! Is Grandma here yet?" she yelled.

"Not yet," said Shelby's mother, "but hurry. Grandma will be at the airport soon."

Shelby zoomed through the house. Baby Hannah toddled after her, trying hard to keep up.

Shelby could hardly sit still
as they drove to the airport.
"May Grandma sleep with me tonight?" she asked.

"Grandma doesn't want to sleep with a wiggle-worm," Shelby's mother said. Shelby frowned. Shelby was a champion wiggleworm.

Shelby wiggled and squiggled and scooted and squirmed all night long. Once she even kerplopped right onto the floor.

"Don't worry, Shelby," her mother said. "At night you can put Grandma in your dreams."

Shelby smiled. In her dreams, she and Grandma would sing Shelby's favorite songs and read storybooks over and over again. She would rock in Grandma's lap, even though Shelby wasn't a baby anymore.

Best of all, Shelby could dream about making cookies with Grandma. Shelby and Grandma were a cookie-making team.

Then Shelby asked, "Mommy, why does Grandma live at the airport?" "Shelby," her mother said, "Grandma doesn't live at the airport. Don't you remember Grandma's house, high in the mountains?"

Shelby did remember being at Grandma's house. At Grandma's, Shelby hiked up the mountain with Grandpa and Nikki dog.

She climbed on the big red rocks. She slid
down a snowy hill on her bright yellow sled.

"An airport is just a place where airplanes park," said Shelby's mother. "Airplanes carry people from one place to another. No one lives at the airport. Look, there is Grandma's plane landing now."

Grandma's plane had taken her over the mountains all the way to Shelby's town.

That night after dinner, Grandma had a surprise. "This is for you, Shelby," she said, "It is a very special map."

ALASKA
WASHINGTON
MONTANA
NORTH DAKOTA
OREGON
IDAHO
SOUTH DAKOTA
WYOMING
NEBRASKA
NEVADA
CALIFORNIA
UTAH
COLORADO
KANSAS
NEW MEXICO
ARIZONA
TEXAS
HAWAII

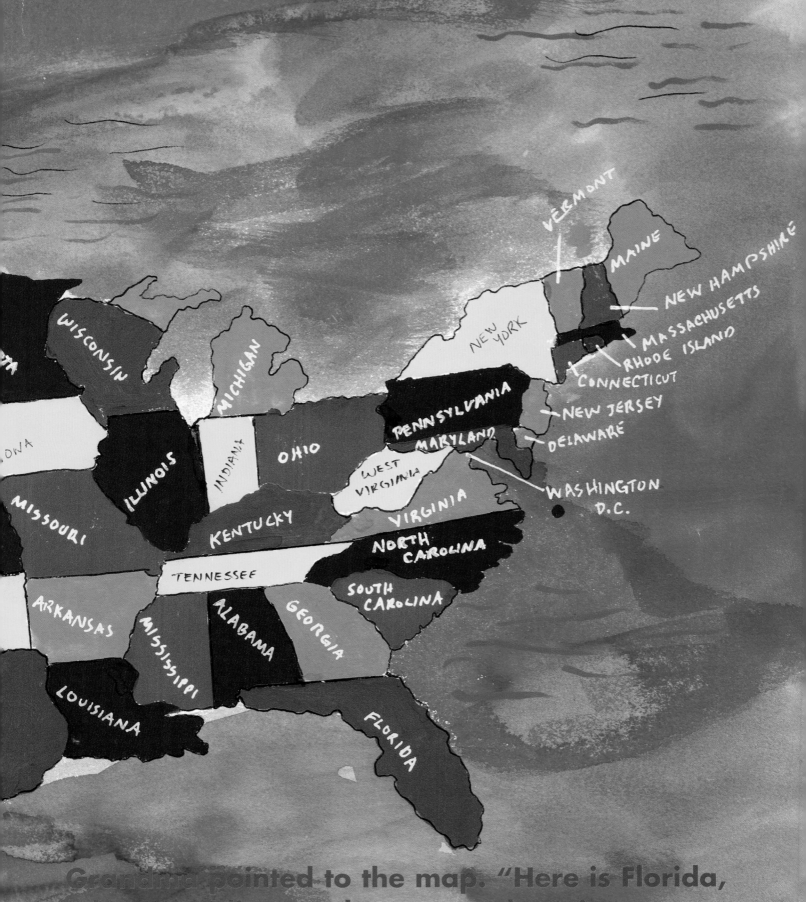

Grandma pointed to the map. "Here is Florida, where you live. And way over here is Colorado, where I live."

Then Grandma opened a big envelope full of photographs. There were Shelby's grandmas and grandpas and aunts and uncles and cousins. Some lived close, and some lived far away.

Shelby watched Grandma place all the pictures on the map until her whole family was spread from one end to the other.
Then Shelby understood. She knew exactly where Grandma lived.

That night Shelby put Grandma in her dreams. Shelby and Grandma sang and rocked and read stories. They even made cookies.

Then Shelby dreamed about all the world's grandmas and grandpas, aunts and uncles and cousins. She dreamed they were high up in the air, flying around in airplanes, going to see the children they loved.

CONTACT:

Red Hill Press

P.O. Box 2053

Carbondale, Colorado 81623

Phone: (970) 963-4968

FAX: (970) 963-6978

Email: redhill@rof.net

Printed in Singapore